WORLD W...

TE...

DEARY

THE BOMBER BALLOON

Illustrated by James de la Rue

BLOOMSBURY EDUCATION
AN IMPRINT OF BLOOMSBURY

LONDON OXFORD NEW YORK NEW DELHI SYDNEY

Chapter 1

DORA and the dog

Peldon, Essex, 24th Sept 1916

Millie Watson screamed. She wasn't afraid of the dark. But when she ran into the man, as solid as a brown-backed bear, she screamed.

She had been running through the dark and empty streets. The gas street lamps were never turned on at night now. 'The balloon bombers will see the lamps and drop their bombs on our house,' her mum had explained as she heated the clothes iron over the fire.

Dad had been sitting at the far side of the fireplace, smoking a pipe and reading the newspaper. 'How many times do I have to tell you, Mrs Watson, they are not balloon bombers – they are Zeppelins.'

'Yes, Mr Watson,' her mother replied, 'but we aren't all clever like you. Some of us don't understand words like zippy-things. All our Millie needs to know is they are big balloons that drop nasty bombs.'

Mr Watson's moustache bristled as he sighed. 'Zeppelins are large frames of wood or metal as long as our street. They are covered with canvas and filled with gas. They are so light they can carry twenty men and fifty bombs.'

Mrs Watson turned from ironing the shirt to Millie. 'He just read that in the paper. He reads that paper and believes every word. Then he repeats it like a parrot to his mates in the pub. They think he's the brainiest bloke in Britain. But really he's just a parrot.'

Mr Watson sniffed and ignored her.

'Squawk, squawk. Who's a pretty boy then?' Mrs Watson said.

Her husband poked at the dusty coal on the fire. 'Time I went to the pub,' he said.

Mrs Watson turned to Millie again. 'We're short of food – not enough bread and butter and milk and eggs to go around. But those men still manage to find beer.'

'I am going to a meeting,' Mr Watson said. 'The Royal Defence group want to talk about DORA.'

'Dora Potts in our class?' Millie asked.

'No, child,' Mrs Watson said. 'Defence Of the Realm Act... D-O-R-A. All the things we have to do, now we are at war. DORA is just rules you have to stick to or the policeman will send you to prison.'

Mr Watson shrugged himself into his coat and placed his cap on his head. 'The people who break the rules will be fined, Mrs Watson – not sent to prison. And the police are too busy to do it, so the men of the town will form a Royal Defence Army.

We will patrol the streets and make sure DORA is obeyed.'

'You'll enjoy that,' Mrs Watson muttered.

'A man must do his duty.'

Mrs Watson folded her arms. 'That's telling us, Millie. But if you ask me, it's just an excuse to go to the pub.'

Mr Watson picked up his newspaper, folded it neatly and slid it into his pocket. 'I will be back later...'

'If a zippy-thing doesn't drop a bomb on your head,' his wife said.

As Mr Watson left she folded her ironing, took up her knitting and clicked away quietly while Millie picked up a book. It was called *The Flower Fairies* and Miss Jepson, her teacher, had let Millie take it home to practise her reading.

'Nice book?' her mum asked.

'Fairies,' Millie said with a sigh. 'The boys get to read proper books about war and fighting. I have to read about fairies.'

Mrs Watson smiled. 'Why not run along to the corner shop on Mersea Road? The woman next door says they are getting some eggs delivered tonight. Take sixpence out of the tea caddy and run and see if you can get us some.'

Millie threw down the book, collected

the silvery coin and raced out of the house into the dark street.

The old man who lit the gas lamps with a long pole never came around the streets now. Not since the war against Germany started. Millie often wondered what had happened to the old man.

Her thin boots were slapping on the pavements, her thinner hair streaming behind her, and her mouth open and panting. Millie loved running.

The houses had heavy curtains at the windows but there was still a glow in the streets. Enough for her to race along the roads without falling.

She dodged around the lampposts and the pillar-boxes and into Church Road. She knew what was coming and giggled as she gasped and ran. There, on the doorstep of number 17, Mac the dog was waiting. A sandy-coloured dog with a tattered ear. A mongrel with a bad temper and a yap like a broken hinge.

Mac heard Millie's slapping soles before she turned the corner and a growl grew in his throat. When he saw the running girl his little black teddy-bear eyes glowed like coals. He leapt forward, yapping madly and snapping at her flying heels.

'Can't catch me!' she screamed. That wasn't true. But Mac wanted to warn her off, not bite her. She knew that when she reached the end of his road he would stop.

Millie turned the corner and backed down Mersea Road, panting and giggling. That was how she walked into the man who was solid as a bear.

And that was when Millie screamed.

Chapter 2

Buttons and bombs

'Now then, now, then, now then,' the man growled. He was almost invisible in the darkness in his uniform of midnight blue. All Millie could see was his pale moon-face and the silver buttons on his jacket.

'Good evening, Constable Smith,' Millie said.

'Young Millie Watson, isn't it?'

'Yes, Constable.'

'Do you realise you have put the whole of Essex in danger, young lady?' he said fiercely.

'Me?' she squeaked. 'How?'

'Shush,' he hissed. 'Look over there, towards Mersea Island. What can you see?'

Fingers of yellow-white light crisscrossed the sky. There were orange flashes sparkling round. 'Ooooh! It's like Bonfire Night,' Millie said. 'Like before the war.'

Constable Smith sighed. 'The lights are searchlights over the Thames – forty or fifty miles away. The flashes are the anti-aircraft shells exploding. Mark my words, there are Zeppelins about tonight. You know what a Zeppelin is?'

Millie nodded. 'They are large frames of wood or metal as long as our street. They are covered with canvas and filled with gas lamps. They are so light they can carry twenty thousand men and fifty thousand bombs.'

Constable Smith coughed. 'Not quite that many, but enough to make a big hole in your house. And do you know how they will find your house?'

'No, Constable Smith.'

'They will find it because they will fly over the town, they will switch off their engines, and they will hear every sound. They will hear that dog barking and say, "Aha! Where there's dogs, there's people". And they'll drop a bomb.'

'On Mac the dog? That's not fair.'

'And it will all be your fault for making him bark. See? Now, have you heard of DORA?' the policeman asked.

'The Defence Of the Rum Act.'

'Realm,' the constable said.

'The rules we have to stick to. If we don't, my dad will send you to prison.'

'Your dad?'

'He's joining the Royal Defence Army. They will arrest people because you policemen are too busy,' she said proudly. 'What are you busy doing?'

'Making sure people stick to DORA rules, of course. Making sure there's nobody hanging around under a railway bridge.'

'We haven't got a railway bridge in this village,' Millie said.

'No... no, but if we *had*, I'd arrest you for hanging around under it. You could be a spy planning to blow it up.'

'A spy?'

'There's lots of them about. That's why DORA says no one can send a letter with invisible ink, and no one can fly a kite.'

'I haven't got a kite,' Millie sighed.

'If you had a kite it could be a signal to other spies,' Constable Smith explained. 'You can't speak in a foreign language on the phone. You must never show a light in the street at night, and you have to keep quiet in the street. There are no church bells after sunset, and it is against the law to whistle in the street.'

'Or make a dog bark after dark?'

'Exactly.' The constable nodded. He spoke softly. 'There could be twenty Germans up there in a Zeppelin, just listening and waiting. Remember that next time you make a silly noise.'

Millie trembled. She wasn't afraid of the dark, but she was afraid of a bomb landing on her head. She whispered, 'Are they there now?'

'No, but they are not far away. See the search-lights? They are moving towards us... and listen!'

'What?'

'Aeroplanes. I can hear aeroplanes.'

Millie strained her ears and heard the faint buzz like distant bees on a summer meadow.

'They've sent up aeroplanes to shoot it down. Mark my words, there's a Zeppelin coming this way.'

Chapter 3
Balloon and beer

Captain Alois Bocker's face was frozen. Frozen with the icy winds at four thousand metres above London, and frozen with fear. He stood in the cabin of Zeppelin L33. His crew of eighteen men were staring at him.

At last Sail-maker Ernst Kaiser spoke. 'What shall we do, sir?'

'Do?' Captain Bocker said, swallowing hard.

'The canvas has torn. The gas is escaping,' Kaiser said.

'Mend it.'

The sail-maker shook his head. 'A piece of shell ripped through it. It is far too big a hole to repair while we are flying, in the dark. We can only do it when we get home.'

'So get us home,' the Captain barked at Steersman Siegfried Korber.

He nodded. 'We head east, then over the English Channel.'

'We are losing height,' Signalman Gustav Kunischt reminded the captain.

Alois Bocker's brain began to work again. 'Throw everything over the side that we don't need – landing ropes, food tins... erm...'

'Bombs?' Sail-maker Kaiser asked.

'Of course.'

'Should we throw Signalman Kunischt over the side?' Steersman Korber asked. Kunischt was round as a barrel, but not quite as heavy as a house.

'Yes, good idea,' Captain Bocker said without thinking. The crew laughed. Captain Bocker managed a thin smile as if he shared the joke. Kunischt didn't think it was funny.

The men were as scared as their captain was. Scared of the word no one spoke. The word *feuer*. Fire. If a spark from the engines met the leaking gas, the balloon would catch fire and they would fall, burning, onto England.

But the shell had not set the balloon alight yet. They had a chance.

The men hurried to throw as much as they could over the side. Their bombs flashed briefly when they struck the distant ground.

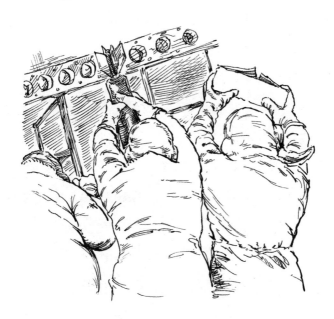

Their hearts rose as the balloon rose. 'We're going to make it.' Steersman Korber smiled, and wiped an oily hand over the sweat on his bald head.

Then he heard the rattle of a machine gun. He turned to peer through the windows of the cabin and saw the glint of bullets streaming over his head.

'Captain, we are under attack from English planes!'

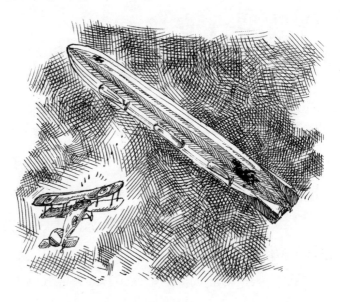

'I can see that, you fool.'

'Your orders, captain?'

'Dive, dive, dive! In the dark he'll never find us again.'

'But if we lose height we'll never get home,' Signalman Kunischt argued.

'I know that, *Dummkopf*. Climb, climb, climb!' the captain shouted.

Engineer Joseph Wegener called back, 'That last attack lost us more gas. We'll never climb.'

'So dive, dive, dive!'

The German airmen crashed into one another as they ran back and forth to obey the changing orders.

'We'll never get home. We'll drown in the sea,' Signalman Kunischt said.

'Then let us land on the ground while we can.'

'We'll be prisoners,' Korber wailed.

Captain Bocker's face was pale with red spots of rage in his cheeks. 'Tell me, Korber, what would you like us to do? Shall we burn in the air, drown in the sea, jump and smash onto the ground – or live the rest of the war in a British prison camp?'

Korber gave a weak smile. 'When you put it like that, Captain...'

'Yes?'

'Show me the way to the prison camp.'

Engineer Wegener said, 'We need to cut the engines so they don't set fire to the balloon when we hit the ground.'

The captain nodded. 'We will land safely and *then* I will set fire to the balloon so the British do not learn the secrets of our Zeppelins.'

He turned to the men in the cabin. 'Ready, men, prepare to land in England. Where will we touch down, Witthoft?' he asked a young man who was squinting at a map.

'The county of Essex,' Witthoft said.

Captain Bocker smiled. 'I have an English cousin in the town of Colchester. He will make sure we are well cared for. Hold tight, *Kameraden*, we are going to drop into England for a pint of their famous beer.'

Chapter 4
Shadows and cycles

In the calm of the night Millie and Constable Smith stood silent, listening. The buzzing of the aeroplanes faded.

Then another, deeper rumble could be heard to the west.

'Zeppelin,' the policeman muttered. 'Headed this way.'

As they strained their ears the drone of the engines stopped.

'That's what you said, Constable Smith.

You said they switch their engines off to listen.'

The policeman nodded. 'And if everyone stays perfectly quiet he may just glide over us.'

Millie felt she was holding her breath forever. She looked up. There was no moon that night but the purple sky was dusted with a billion burning stars. Suddenly a shadow blotted out a few million of them as the Zeppelin sank towards them.

Constable Smith saw it a few moments after Millie. 'He's too low to drop bombs,' he gasped. 'If he drops a bomb now it'll explode underneath him and blow him out of the sky.'

'So what's he doing?' Millie squeaked.

The monster shadow shone a dull starlight silver as it passed over their heads and they heard a whistling. The air caught in the ragged rips of the canvas and sighed as if the Zeppelin was giving a dying-animal cry... which it was.

'It's crashing!' the policeman shouted, loud enough to break the DORA rules, and for a moment wondered if he should arrest himself.

His boots clattered over the cobbled road and sparks flew from the nails in the soles. 'Where are you going?' Millie asked, sprinting after him. He didn't reply.

She raced past Mac the ginger dog, who was too frightened by the sky-shadow to bark. Constable Smith hammered at the door of the house at the end of the row. When the door flew open he panted, 'Special Constable Elijah Taylor, get your uniform and your bike – there's a German airship landing. I reckon she'll touch down about two miles to the west.'

Taylor was a tall old man, as thin as his bicycle frame. He scrambled for his uniform and his cycle and was still fastening buttons as he wobbled down the road. There were two cycles outside the police station and Constable Smith leapt onto one. Millie grabbed the other and followed. It was too big for her but if she stood up she could just reach the pedals.

Elijah Taylor looked over his shoulder. 'Go home. This is no place for a girl.'

'I'm not a girl,' Millie answered. 'I'm a member of the Royal Defence Army. And I'm going to arrest a German.'

'You're too young,' he groaned as he pedalled.

'You're too old,' Millie argued. 'If you can do it so can I.'

Constable Smith gave a wild laugh. 'She's right, Elijah. She'll be more use than you.'

34

'How?' the old man asked angrily.

'You'll see,' Constable Smith said. 'You'll see.'

The bicycles hummed along the quiet roads between high hedges and fields full of sheep and cows. The air was warm and scented with late summer flowers. Millie felt as far away from the war as those stars.

Then she heard the creak of Constable Smith's brakes and his cycle skidded to a halt. Though a gap in the hedge she could see why he had stopped. An amber light spilled across the fields from the village of Little Wigborough.

'Ah, they have crashed in flames,' Elijah Taylor said. 'There won't be any Germans for us to arrest.'

But Special Constable Taylor was wrong.

Chapter 5

Barns and babies

Zeppelin L33 had floated down like a dandelion seed towards the waiting fields of England. As the gas leaked it began to gather speed.

The men braced themselves against the sides of the cabin and held on to one another.

The balloon rushed down over Farmer George Eldon's barn and took off the weather-vane. Luckily, Farmer Eldon had just ploughed his field so the Zeppelin landed in soft, crumbling soil.

The crunched landing led to a few sprains, several cuts and lots of bruises, but no one died. Captain Alois Bocker pushed open the cabin door and stumbled down onto enemy soil. 'Everyone out, quickly,' he ordered, and the men scrambled past him onto the ploughed soil. Then he called, 'Engineer Wegener?'

'Yes, sir?' the broomstick-thin young man with dark eyes asked.

'Open the fuel tanks and let the petrol out. Fill a bucket with the petrol and make a trail like a fuse to the machine. I need to set it on fire so the British do not get the secrets of the Zeppelins.'

'Yes, sir,' Engineer Wegener said and hurried to obey.

Signalman Kunischt rolled his barrel-body back to his captain. 'We are very close to that row of farm cottages, sir, and

they have thatch on the roof. When we set fire to the Zeppelin we could burn the houses and barns. There could be cattle in the barns.'

'A good point, Kunischt. Get the men lined up on the road ready to march. I will deal with this problem,' the captain said. He dusted down his uniform and put his cap straight before marching over to the cottage door. He raised a hand and knocked hard.

A dog barked. There was the scrape of a chair as it was jammed under the handle to keep out the stranger. Captain Bocker spoke in perfect English. 'Good evening. I am sorry to disturb you.'

The dog barked. 'Good evening, sir,' the German went on. 'Are you there?'

'No,' came the fast reply in a shaking voice.

'You say there is no one there?' repeated the German.

'No. I'm not here. I'm in the pub.'

Captain Bocker took a deep breath. 'Is this one of your English jokes?'

'I'm not laughing,' the farmer said. 'I have a shotgun and I'll use it.' His voice wobbled.

The Zeppelin captain stepped aside so any blast from a shotgun would miss him. 'I simply wish to tell you that my airship has landed in the field at the back of this house.'

'I just ploughed that field,' the man behind the door grumbled.

'I am about to set fire to it.'

'To my field?'

'To my airship. But I wanted to warn you that sparks may fly and set fire to your house or barn.'

'Are you one of those bomber-balloon blokes?' the voice asked.

'*Ja.*'

'You drop bombs on women and babies?'

'We cannot help that.'

'And you're worried about my old cottage?'

'*Ja.*'

'Well, why aren't you worried about the people you drop bombs on?' the man asked.

Captain Bocker sighed. 'When you are four thousand metres in the air you do not think of the people below as people. They are just targets.'

'And you will be a target if I fire this shotgun through the door.'

The German sighed again. 'Good night to you, sir. It has been a pleasure talking to you.'

'You too,' came the reply. 'Go carefully now.'

'I will.' The German airship captain wandered down the path to the main road where his men waited.

'Are you all right, sir?' Signalman Kunischt asked.

'I don't know. I think we landed next to a madhouse.' He shook his head. 'Engineer Wegener, light the petrol trail. Destroy the balloon. The rest of you... quick march!'

Chapter 6

Cowards and kids

Millie and the two policemen heard the sound of tramping boots and pulled on the brakes of their cycles. Special Constable Elijah Taylor said, 'That'll be the army on the way to the crash to see if there are any Germans left.'

'No,' Constable Smith said. 'The army are three miles away on Mersea Island. They couldn't get here that quick.'

'So who are they?' Millie asked breathlessly. The crunch of the boots on the ancient road was closer now.

'Let's ask them, shall we?' the constable said. He turned on his bicycle lamp and the marching men saw it. They clattered to an untidy halt.

Captain Bocker stepped forward. 'Good evening,' he said politely, but his hand was resting on the pistol at his belt.

'Good evening, sir,' the policeman replied. 'And where are you off to?'

'Colchester,' Bocker said. 'It's not far, is it?'

'Six miles, sir.'

'And is this the right road?' the German asked.

'It is, sir. If you would care to follow me?'

The policemen and Millie turned their cycles towards Peldon and wheeled them ahead of the Zeppelin crew.

'Where are we going?' Millie hissed.

'Peldon,' Constable Smith said.

'I know, but why?'

'Because there is a telephone in Peldon and a few more special constables.'

'There's Fairhead, Clement Hyam, Charlie King, Joseph May, Horace Meade, Harry Beade and Edgar Nicholas,' Special Constable Taylor said.

'That's right. Do you know any of them, Millie?'

'Of course,' she said. 'They're nearly all in this Royal Defence Army. They'll be in the pub with my dad.'

'That's right. So when we get to the village I'll go to the telephone box and call the army on Mersea Island. You run off to the pub and get the constables.'

'What about me?' old Elijah Taylor asked.

'You guard them while I make the call.'

Elijah made a choking sound. 'What if that German pulls his pistol?' he gasped.

'He won't,' Millie said. 'Just tell him I'm bringing all the farmers from the pub and they all have shotguns for the crows. He'll end up as dead as the crows if he shoots you.'

'I'll end up deader,' Elijah grumbled.

But it wasn't Elijah Taylor who was in danger. It was Millie.

When they reached the village green Constable Smith stopped and shone his torch on the Germans. 'Now, gentlemen, if you would just wait here I will call for some lorries to give you a lift.'

'You will get us a lift to Colchester?' Captain Bocker asked.

'That's right,' Constable Smith said quietly. He marched across to the telephone box and began to call the army base.

Elijah Taylor turned to the girl. 'Millie, you know what to do.'

But as Millie walked over the dark grass the Zeppelin captain reached out and grabbed her arm. 'And where is the girl going?'

'Bed,' Elijah said quickly. 'It's way past her bedtime and she shouldn't be out.'

Captain Bocker gave a short laugh. 'She can stay up a little longer. We will take her as our hostage. When we are safely on the lorries and on our way to Colchester I will release her.'

'And if he doesn't?' Millie asked, twisting in his grasp.

The Captain sighed and drew the pistol from his belt. 'I will have to shoot you.'

Even in the darkness Millie's face seemed to glow with anger. She turned to the airship crew whose pale faces loomed in the gloom. 'Do you speak English?'

Most of the men muttered, '*Ja.*'

'Is this man your leader?'

'*Ja,*' Signalman Kunischt said.

'Then I feel sorry for you all. Your leader is a coward and a bully. He would shoot a little girl just to save his own skin.'

The men's faces seemed to be pointing down at the cropped grass on the village green.

'I bet some of you have kids,' Millie said.

'*Ja*, we have *kinder,*' Steersman Korber said.

'Would you want one of your children shot by a British soldier?' Millie demanded. Silence.

Finally Engineer Wegener spoke.

'You cannot harm her, Captain. We will surrender. We will be prisoners for a while. When we win the war our friends will set us free. But we do not want the blood of a child on our hands. We could never wash it off.'

Chapter 7
Mac and matches

Captain Bocker shook his head and gave up. 'As you say, we will win this war soon and be free again. Very well, Englishman. Lead me to your prison camp.'

Millie sprinted off to the village pub, the Plough. Moments later the special constables spilled out onto the village green. They formed a line behind the Germans to stop them escaping into the warm darkness. After their freezing trip and miserable crash the German crew did not want to escape anywhere.

Captain Bocker ordered the Zeppelin crew to get into a line ready to march. Constable Smith came out of the phone box and said, 'I'll take your gun, sir, if you don't mind.'

Bocker stood straight and raised his chin. 'I am an officer of the German Army. I will only surrender to a British Army officer.'

Constable Smith shrugged. 'I'm sure we can manage that, sir. Now if you would just march your men this way.' He pointed to the Mersea Island road. The Germans moved into the darkness followed by the constables on foot or on cycles. Millie handed her cycle to Constable Horace Meade and sighed.

Millie's father had come out of the pub to watch the action. 'Time you were home, young lady,' he said.

'But Dad, I want to see how it all ends.'

'You'll see your pillow and nothing else,' he grumbled and pushed her towards their home.

She had to wait till next morning to hear the full story. Elijah Taylor knocked on the kitchen door and Mrs Watson invited him in for a cup of tea. 'We met the British troops about a mile down the road and handed the prisoners over. It was all very quiet. No fuss at all. You didn't miss much, Millie.'

'Our Millie was never there, was she? I only sent her out for a bag of eggs. Her father said she was on the green.'

Elijah Taylor grinned a gap-toothed grin. 'Your Millie only went and – '

'Watched!' Millie put in. 'I only watched on my way back from the shop.' If her mum ever heard of the girl having a pistol pointed to her head she would never be allowed out of the house at night again.

The constable nodded. 'That's right,' he said. 'No danger at all.'

'Constable Smith was very brave,' Millie said.

'He's not Constable Smith any more,' Elijah said. 'They told him he will be a sergeant now. And they're going to give him a merit badge. He's as happy as a dog with three tails.'

Millie's mum turned to her. 'All that excitement in Peldon and we missed it all.'

'Yes, Mum,' Millie said and hid her smile.

* * *

When the autumn winds started to sweep the streets of the village with crackling leaves. Millie's eyes scoured the skies for bomber balloons but none ever came that way again. Sometimes she would see the searchlights chasing clouds over London, fifty miles away.

Then she would turn and race along the coal-dark, cold, dark streets. Mac spent his evenings in front of the fire these days. But one night he surprised her. As she turned to run past his house he was there on the step. His barks split the quiet air.

'Shush, Mac, the Zeppelins will hear you,' she squeaked. She turned the corner, and walked into the man who was solid as a bear.

'Sorry, Constable Smith – I mean Sergeant Smith,' she said. 'Please don't lock me up! I didn't know Mac would be there tonight.'

The round-faced, ruddy-cheeked policeman smiled. 'Lock up a brave young girl like you? Why no. The girl that stood up to a Zeppelin captain? I should think not.'

'I haven't told Mum or Dad what happened that night,' she said.

'I know.' The policeman nodded. 'I knew those Germans wouldn't shoot a girl – that's why I let you come along. I shouldn't have done it, I know. So it will stay our secret, eh?'

'And you won't arrest me?'

The man threw back his head and gave a deep chuckle. 'No, no. I've done my arresting for tonight.'

'You arrested a German?'

'No an Englishman. He broke the DORA rules. I saw him come out of the Plough pub on the green,' the policeman explained.

'Did he shout out, or slam a door, or whistle in the street, or fly a kite?'

'No, he struck a match to light his pipe.'

'He didn't!' Millie gasped.

'A Zeppelin overhead could have seen that. I arrested him on the spot and he'll appear in Colchester court tomorrow morning. We can't have people striking matches in the street.'

'No, sergeant. That's shocking,' Millie agreed, then she ran off home.

'I'm back, Mum,' she cried as she burst through the door. 'And I got three eggs.'

'Shush,' Mrs Watson said. 'Keep your voice down. We don't want to upset your dad.'

Mr Watson sat in the chair, staring into the fire with a face like a midnight cloud. Millie whispered, 'What's wrong with him, Mum?'

Mrs Watson took her into the kitchen and said quietly, 'He's upset. He's been very silly and got himself in a lot of trouble.'

'What did he do?'

'He struck a match to light his pipe in the street,' Mrs Watson said.

Did you know?

Count Ferdinand Zeppelin, a German army officer, started building airships in 1897. The German army started using them in 1909. At the start of the First World War the German Army had seven Zeppelins.

The first Zeppelin raid on London was on 31st May 1915. The attack killed 28 people and injured 60 more.

On 24th Sept 1916 Zeppelin L-33 of this story was under the command of Captain Alois Bocker. It was shot down and landed near New Hall Cottages, Little Wigborough. Bocker knocked on the doors of the cottages to warn the people he was going to set fire to the machine. But the fire didn't destroy the Zeppelin and the British balloon builders learned a lot form the wreck.

Bocker marched his men towards Colchester but he was met by Constable Charles

Smith. The constable stopped the German crew and called the army. With the help of the Special Constables in the village the Germans were led towards Mersea Island where the army took them prisoner. From that day the policeman was known as 'Zepp' Smith. He died in 1977 at the age of 94.

In Britain the DORA law ordered that no lights could be shown after dark. In 1916, in York, the first person fined was Jim Richardson, who was fined 5 shillings for lighting a cigarette in the street at night.

115 Zeppelins were used during the war but 77 were shot down and many more lost in accidents. There had been 51 raids in which 5,806 bombs were dropped, killing 557 people and injuring 1,358. The Zeppelins were called 'Baby-killers' by the British people, but were too easy to hit with guns and aeroplanes and the last raid took place in June 1917.

The war ended in November 1918.

What next?

1. The Defence of the Realm Act (DORA) made new laws. Some seem odd.

'You must NOT hang around under a railway bridge'. (You could be plotting to blow it up).

'You must not fly a kite.' (You could be a spy and the kite could be a signal)

'You must not whistle in the street'. (A Zeppelin could hear you and drop bombs).

If you were head teacher of your school what five new Defence of the School Act (DOSA) rules would you have?

2. Zeppelins wrecked a lot of buildings, leaving big spaces in many city centres. Later, new buildings were put up in their place. What would you do if you could plan the buildings in your area? Would you knock any building down? Write a letter to the Leader of your Council. Say which building you want the council to demolish. Say why. Say what you would put in its place.

3. Imagine you are at school in 1915 in the First World War. As you leave school you see a man or a woman climb down from the roof of your school. They have put a white sheet there so the zeppelins can see it and bomb it. Draw a 'Wanted' poster that shows the spy and describe them below. (Reward £100 by the way.)